February

Dear Jennifer and Lauren,
I hope you like this book.
Love,
Lydia Boruta

Lauren. Jennifer
Love.

Kenneth Grahame's
The Wind
in the
Willows

Kenneth Grahame's
The Wind in the Willows

Retold by Lornie Leete-Hodge
Illustrated by Ronald Embleton

DEAN

Originally published in England by Deans International Publishing.
Published in United States and simultaneously in Canada by Joshua Morris, Inc.
167 Old Post Road
Southport, CT 06490
Copyright © Deans International Publishing.
A division of the Hamlyn Publishing Group, 1985
All Rights Reserved

ISBN 0-887-05117-0

Made and printed in Great Britain by
Purnell and Sons (Book Production) Ltd.,
Member of the BPCC Group, Paulton, Bristol

The Wind in the Willows

A pale sun made little ripples on the dark waters of the slow-moving river, and on its banks the animals stirred and busied themselves. It was the first day of spring and there was much to do to shake off the cold, dark days of winter and plan for the year ahead. The grass and reeds were showing tiny shoots of green, and the trees were tipped with buds. It was still cold but the brightness told everyone it was time to start the new season.

Otter pushed through a clump of weeds to look at the river. It was moving faster now, speckling over the stones, with here and there a fish darting in a silver flash.

Far beneath the riverbank, Mole was stirring himself. He was a small, timid creature and a wonderful burrower, his sleek black-furred body perfect for pushing through the earth. Like all moles he had built himself a sort of fortress to live in and was very proud of it. He had spent hours digging and burrowing for he liked it to be just right.

"Hey, ho," he said, yawning, "there's a lot to do and no time for dawdling."

And he busied himself with brush and pan, dusters and mops. He liked his little home to be spick and span and, no matter how often he cleaned it, there always seemed to be dust somewhere!

As the day wore on, Mole's home shone with a brightness that told him it was time to go and see the spring for himself. He gently pushed his way along the tunnels he had made, until at last his little pink nose emerged into the sunlight. Blinking, he looked around to see if it was safe, then climbed out on to the cool grass of the meadow.

"Oh, this is lovely," he said, squirming his dark glossy body over and over. He could hear the birds singing and the river running and clapped his tiny pink paws in delight.

Mole stood up and shook himself, patting his sleek fur into place for he was proud of his thick dark coat. Whichever way he rubbed it, it stayed sleek and flat, unlike some of the other animals whose coats were all spiky and rough no matter how much they smoothed them.

"Hello Rabbit," he called cheerily to a passing rabbit, but he was in a hurry.

"Hello Mole," he said. "Can't stop now, too much to do. Nice to see you."

So Mole continued on his way. How lovely it all was, he thought. It was the best time of the whole year. Never before had he strayed so far from his fortress. Usually he poked his little face out, greeted anyone who was passing and hurried back inside. Today he felt different. Brave.

It was all very exciting. Mole was on the riverbank. He sat and watched the other side as the river flowed by. He could just see, for his eyes were small and weak, something moving in the reeds opposite. Something bright and shiny. Could it be a star? he wondered. Then, with a sort of whoosh, a head appeared. A little brown face, with small, neat ears and whiskers. It was Water Rat!

"Hello Mole, old friend," said Rat, waving a paw.

"Hello Rat, how are you?" squeaked Mole.

"Come on over," invited Rat. "We'll have a talk."

"But I can't," wailed Mole, for he longed to cross over but didn't swim. And the other side was so far away.

Rat looked at him. Then he untied a rope and gave a good, strong pull. To Mole's surprise a little boat came out of the reeds. Rat stepped lightly into it, picked up the oars and in a trice had crossed the river and was by his side.

"Come on then," said Rat, "it's quite safe."

But Mole had never seen a boat before. He looked at the small boat in delight. "It's blue and white," he said, clapping his paws together.

"Yes, yes," said Rat. "Come along do." He held up a paw to help Mole over the side. "Steady now," he cautioned. "Don't rock the boat."

Mole sat on the seat and looked all round him. "This is the most wonderful day of my life," he said, his eyes shining. He looked this way and that, he just couldn't believe it was real.

Rat took an oar and pushed the boat away from the bank. A few strong pulls on the oars and they were on the other side of the river, and Rat, leaping out, was tying the rope to a tree branch.

"Come on," he said, holding out a paw to help Mole.

"Just a minute," begged Mole. "This is the most exciting day of my life! I'd never seen a boat before, and now I've *seen* one and *been* in one!"

"Never been in a boat before?" Rat was amazed.

Mole leant back in his seat. The boat was perfect to him with its blue and white paint, the cushions and shiny gleam of the oars, wet from the river. "Oh, this is magic!" he sighed.

"Magic!" scoffed Rat. "It's the *only* thing." He leaned forward, "Come on Mole, I tell you the river is the only place to live and there is nothing, absolutely *nothing* as wonderful as messing about in boats."

Mole felt the boat sway a little and suddenly he wanted to be on dry land. He leapt up and the boat rocked and tilted.

"Ooh," squeaked Mole, now very scared.

"Come on, it's quite safe," said Rat, helping the trembling Mole over the side.

And, having tied the boat safely to the branch, put the oars away, and covered the seats, just in case it rained, Rat led the way to his home.

Rat opened the front door and Mole followed him into the house. It was bigger than his fortress with lots of rooms, all spick and span, with everything just in its place. "Come on in," said Rat. "Make yourself at home."

Rat went into his neat kitchen and Mole crept in after him. There was so much to see. How he envied Rat the wooden dresser with its rows of blue and white china, each one with a small picture of a rat on it. How dull his own white plates seemed! Gingerly, he picked up one of the plates and looked at it.

"Why, there's a picture of you on every one!" he cried, unable to believe his eyes.

Rat laughed. "Well not exactly *me*," he said, "just Water Rats. Some of them do look like me," and he smoothed his fine whiskers, "but all of us Water Rats have these plates. Some have red ones but

I like blue best. As you noticed, my boat is blue and white."

Rat made Mole a cup of tea and offered him a delicious muffin. There was so much to talk about, and so many questions Mole wanted to ask.

"I've lived on the riverbank all my life," said Rat, leaning back in his favourite chair.

"It's all new to me," said Mole. "Who else lives here?"

Rat looked at him. "You don't know much, do you," he said. "Never mind, I'll tell you all about my other friends."

Mole felt very pleased. It was good to be one of Rat's friends and he wanted to stay for ever and hear all about the other river people. It was a new and exciting world to him, and he wriggled his toes in delight.

"My nearest neighbour is Otter," said Rat. "He's very friendly and so useful."

"Useful?" interrupted Mole. How could Otter be *useful*?

"He's a very fast swimmer," said Rat, "and he knows the river so well, he takes any messages for us. And he always knows all that goes on. Don't you wish you could swim as he does—in and out in a flash?"

Mole didn't answer. He couldn't swim at all.

"There are the birds," Rat went on. "Some of them, like the moorhens and dabchicks live, like us, on the river. Soon you will see them with their chicks swimming along in a brood. We don't have any swans now. They are beautiful white birds, so big and strong." He paused to give Mole some more tea and another muffin.

On and on he talked, telling the entranced Mole all about the

river and its people. Mole could have stayed for ever, but he knew
he must return to his little home. Suddenly he did not want to go, it
was so cosy with Rat, and his home often seemed very empty.

"Well, I must be getting back," he said, getting up. "Thank you
for a lovely ride and tea and everything."

"Not at all, not at all," said Rat. "What are friends for?" Then,
as he was a very kind animal, and he knew Mole wanted to stay
very much, he said, "But there's no need for you to go. I'd be glad
of your company. You can stay as long as you like, plenty of spare
rooms. Come and see. After all, friends are special." And Rat took
Mole all round his home. "You can sleep in this room, or this one,
whichever you like," he said.

Mole looked at the rooms, each bed neatly made and so inviting.
He *wanted* to stay here more than anything in the world. He chose
the room with the blue bedspread. He liked blue best of all. Rat's
boat was blue and that was magic to him.

So Mole stayed with Rat and every day they walked along the
riverbank or, treat of treats, Rat took Mole for a ride in his boat.

The sun shone, the birds nested in the trees and the river was
busy with the sounds of summer. The moorhen and her chicks
swam in the river and Otter was teaching his cubs how to swim and
fish.

Mole enjoyed every day and had long stopped feeling he should go home. As for kindly Rat, he liked Mole too much to want him to leave.

"I know," said Rat one fine morning, "let's have a picnic today."

"A picnic," exclaimed Mole, clapping his paws, "what's that?"

"Why, we'll take some food and eat it somewhere along the riverbank," said Rat. "I know the perfect place."

He opened a cupboard and took out a large basket. Mole watched, fascinated. The basket was filled with blue and white plates, blue and white knives and forks and cups. Rat then made some sandwiches, filling them with all Mole's favourite foods. He wrapped them carefully in a cloth to keep them fresh and packed them in the basket. He added some chocolate biscuits in a tin, some fruit and a big bottle of lemonade. The picnic was ready. Rat took a large blue rug (it had to be blue of course) from a drawer and handed it to Mole. "You carry this," he said, "I'll bring the rest." And, tucking the basket under his arm, he shut the door tightly and they set off.

"Hang on a minute," Rat said. "Let me put the food in the boat first."

So Mole waited on the riverbank, almost jumping up and down with excitement.

"Right," said Rat, holding out a paw to help Mole aboard. The basket was stowed under the seat and Mole put the rug beside it as he sat down. "We're off," said Rat, and with a few strong pulls on the oars the little blue and white boat moved smoothly on the shining water.

As they glided along in the warm sunshine, Rat and Mole called out greetings to Otter and his family, and Rabbit who was busy as usual. The river widened as Rat moved on and then at last he came to a little lake with a high bank. He pulled in, tied up the boat, then leapt ashore and turned to give Mole a hand.

"This is it," he said. "We'll have our picnic here."

Mole handed the basket to Rat and then scrambled out of the boat. "It's a good place," said Rat. "We can watch the river from here."

Rat opened the basket, put out the blue and white plates and unwrapped the sandwiches. "Help yourself," he said, taking one himself. "Eat as many as you like."

So, for a time, neither said a word. They were too busy eating. Then, when neither could eat another bite, Rat leaned back and began to talk.

"I always come here in the summer," he said. "It's a fine place for a picnic and you can see most of our stretch of the water. See, there's Otter teaching his eldest to fish over there! And those silly moorhens swimming along in a line, with the youngest always getting left behind!" And he pointed with his paw.

Mole looked all around him. "There's the rabbits," he offered, "and all those birds making such a noise!"

Rat nodded. He'd seen it all before. And, truth to tell, he was feeling just the teeniest bit sleepy. A nap, and he'd be ready to row home.

But Mole was curious. "What is on the other side?" he asked. He could see tall trees and it all looked very big and strange.

Rat opened an eye. "Oh, that's the Wild Wood," he said shortly. "We riverbankers don't go there."

"Why?" Mole *had* to know.

"Well, some of the animals there aren't very nice," said Rat. "The bushy-tailed squirrels that live in the trees—they're all right, great nut eaters. The rabbits, well you know them. And then there's Owl, but you won't see him for he only comes out at night. There's Badger, of course. He lives in the middle of the Wild Wood. Dear Badger, but don't annoy him or interfere with him," he warned. "Nobody does that."

"But why should anyone interfere with him?" asked Mole, not really sure what it meant.

"There's the foxes, they're all right, I'm friends with them," said Rat. "It's the weasels and stoats you can't trust. Don't have anything to do with them, ever—or the ferrets."

Mole was silent. He certainly wouldn't have anything to do with weasels, stoats or ferrets. "Does the Wild Wood go on for ever?" he asked.

"No, of course not," said Rat. "Beyond that is the Wide World,

somewhere that you or I will never visit, so forget about it."

Rat began gathering up the picnic things, stacking the plates and knives in the basket. He had saved a few sandwiches and, going to the edge of the bank, called to Otter who was swimming nearby. "Otter, a treat for you," and he tossed them into the water.

It was time to go home. What a wonderful picnic it had been. Rat was soon rowing swiftly downstream with Mole looking all around him. He had never been so happy. Then he had an idea.

"Rat, I wonder ... that is, do you think...?" and he stopped, afraid to go on.

"What is it?" asked Rat, rowing hard.

"Could I try and row?" said Mole all in a rush.

Rat was doubtful, but he was a kindly rat and Mole was his friend. "All right then," he said. "Easy does it, and don't rock the boat."

Mole was so eager, he stood up, and in a moment had fallen in the water, and he could not swim!

Rat quickly dived in and helped the frightened Mole back into the boat, wrapping the blue rug round him.

"Never mind, soon have you home and dry," he said.

All too soon the picnic was over and the wet and shivering Mole was back in Rat's house sitting by the fire. Rat made him some warm soup and lent him some dry clothes, and soon he felt right as rain.

"Sorry," he said humbly. Rat laughed, "Think nothing of it," he said. "Try again another day."

But Mole never wanted to row again.

And Rat, who was a kindly friend, told Mole all about another friend, Toad, who lived in a big house, Toad Hall.

"Toad is one of our friends," he said, "but we don't see much of him. He's very rich and very spoilt. He lives in a big house, with huge gates. They have stone lions on either side, and there is a long, long drive with trees all the way to the house. It's a fine place for anyone to live." And he put another log on the fire in case Mole should catch cold.

"Toad always does just as he likes," Rat went on, "but however cross we get with him, and we often do, there's something likeable about him all the same."

"May I meet him?" asked Mole who liked the sound of him.

"Why not?" said Rat. "We'll take a walk and see if he is at home, maybe tomorrow."

So, next day, Rat and Mole set off along the river in Rat's boat, waving to the moorhens and Otter as they passed.

"Another picnic?" called Otter hopefully. Those sandwiches had been a treat!

"Not today," said Rat, "looking for Toad."

"Give him my best wishes," called Otter laughing. "No one quite like him."

Rat stopped rowing and pulled into the shore, tying up the boat.

"Come on," he said to Mole, "this is the way."

They set off across the meadow to the road. Soon they heard a strange noise. Clip, clop, rumble, rattle, clip, clop, rumble, rattle. What could it be? Coming towards them, pulled by an old horse, was a gypsy caravan with Toad in the driving seat!

"Hello Toad," Rat called out. "We were on our way to see you!"

Toad waved and pulled hard at the horse's reins. "Whoa!" he cried and the horse stopped, her head hanging. She was glad of a rest.

"Well, what do you think of it?" asked Toad, stepping down and pointing at the caravan. "Smart, isn't it?"

Rat said nothing for a moment. He stood, staring at the caravan which was painted a bright yellow and had four red wheels. He had never seen anything like it in his whole life.

"It's real gypsy," went on Toad, "and the horse, Bessie, is meant to wear this hat," he waved a straw hat, "but it keeps slipping off."

Then Rat remembered Mole who was by his side. "Toad," he said firmly, "this is my friend, Mole." And he pushed Mole forward to shake Toad by the hand. Mole was just the teeniest bit scared of Toad who was dancing round them in a quite excitable manner.

"Glad to know any friend of Ratty," Toad said smiling, and he did not seem so fearsome. "Why not come aboard and have a ride?"

It was pleasant rolling along in the sunshine and Rat and Mole sat back to enjoy the ride. Toad was full of stories of his doings, the friends who had been to stay at the Hall, and how he could not resist buying the caravan when he saw it.

Rat shook his head. "Oh Toad," he said, "what shall we do with you?" But he smiled as he said it for he was very fond of Toad.

The miles went by and Mole began to feel sleepy. Then he was nearly deafened by a terrible noise.

"Toooot! Toooot! Poooop! Pooooop!" And a great roaring sound. He clutched at Rat and they both jumped down to the ground as a huge car sped past, tooting and blaring, with shouts of laughter from the driver and his friends.

Poor Bessie was terrified and reared up, so that Toad fell into the road. He picked himself up and stood staring in happy amazement at the speeding car in the distance.

"My, oh my!" he exclaimed. "Have you ever seen anything like it in your life?"

But Rat and Mole were too busy trying to soothe poor Bessie who was backing steadily into a deep ditch. "There, there," said Rat who couldn't think of anything else to say. But it was no use. Bessie was upset and backed straight down into the ditch, the caravan smashing into pieces.

"Toad, come and help us," called Rat sharply. Toad sadly left the road and helped them to pull poor Bessie from the ditch and unhitch the shafts which were all that remained of the lovely bright caravan that lay broken at the bottom of the ditch.

At last the horse was quiet and Rat, remembering he had a sweet in his pocket, tore off the paper and handed it to Bessie. It wasn't a sugar lump but it was the next best thing.

"Did you ever see anything like that car?" breathed Toad who was very excited.

"Nasty, noisy thing," said Rat who was feeling annoyed. "Come on Toad, we'd best get Bessie back to her stable. There's nothing left of the caravan." And he took Bessie's reins and led her along the hot, dusty road towards Toad Hall, Mole at his heels. Toad took one last look at the ruins of his once loved caravan and set off towards his home. All he wanted now was a car. He just *had* to have a car of his own. What fun he would have, what power!

At last they reached the Hall and Toad remembered his duties as host. "Come in, dear friends," he said. "We must all have some food." And soon they were sitting down to the most scrumptious meal Mole had ever eaten. His eyes nearly popped at the splendour of the Hall, but Rat had seen it all before. Toad toyed with his food. He had a glazed look in his eyes.

Rat saw the danger signals. "Come on Toad," he said briskly, "you can soon find another caravan."

"*Caravan!*" Toad almost shouted. "I'm never going to drive a caravan again. I'm going to have one of those lovely shining *fast* cars!"

"But you can't drive," protested Rat, feeling cross.

"Who cares?" Toad was determined.

Rat and Mole went to the stables to see that Bessie was all right and as Rat patted her head in a kindly way she looked at him in the hope that he might give her another sweet, but it had been his last one.

Soon the two friends were back in Rat's boat and he was rowing towards home. It had been a day Mole would always remember.

For a few days Rat and Mole were busy in the house, but one morning Otter swam up to tell them the latest news.

"Have you heard about Toad?" he asked.

They shook their heads. With Toad anything could happen.

"He went up to London by train today and bought himself a car!" Otter said. "It's coming this week." He *loved* to be the first with any news.

Rat shook his head again. "No good will come of it," he said, and he and Mole began stocking up the store cupboards. The days were shorter and autumn was here.

Mole thought he should go home but Rat wanted him to stay. He wanted to meet Badger but every time he suggested it, Rat made an excuse. "Badger will come here one day," he would say, "just you see. You must not take him *as* you find him, but *when* you find him."

And with that Mole had to be content. He had asked if Rat could not invite Badger to come to the house, just once, but Rat had said he hated parties and that sort of thing.

The evenings grew dark and the rains came and the river was full, so Rat and Mole spent much time indoors. The boat was laid up on the shore. Rat liked to sleep a lot in the winter and Mole was just a bit bored. He stared out at the rain and wished he could do something exciting. Just once! Then he had an idea. Why shouldn't he go to see Badger all by himself?

As usual, Rat was fast asleep, so Mole put on a scarf to keep out the cold and set off across the meadow one afternoon. He knew the way to the Wild Wood, and would go to see Badger and come back

and tell Rat all about it. He quickened his step across the bare and leafless ground. It was very cold and the wind blew his sleek fur.

He had never seen the countryside so bare and it was a strange feeling so he walked faster. Before he knew it, Mole was inside the Wild Wood! Twigs snapped under his feet, and when he turned to see which way to go, he tripped over fallen logs that lay in his path. The tree stumps looked strange, the leaves and fungus growing on them looking like faces, and the tree branches, bare of leaves, seemed to reach out to touch him as he hurried past.

Then he saw the watchers. At first he took no notice, passing the bright gleam of an eye without thought. Then he remembered how Rat had warned him about the weasels and stoats in the Wild Wood. He ran faster and faster, but they seemed to be all around him. He was very scared. There seemed to be a face staring at him from every hole in the banks, so he ran deeper into the wood to get away. His blood froze. He heard a faint whistling which grew louder and louder and then a pattering sound, as if hundreds of little feet were marching after him. His own feet made skittery sounds on the dry leaves and he ran and ran, bumping into trees and logs and brambles. A rabbit brushed past him, its fur soft against his face. "Hide!" it hissed as it disappeared.

At last, Mole found a hollow in an old beech tree and lay there cowering with fright. He was too tired to run any further. If only he had listened to Rat.

Meanwhile, Rat was fast asleep at home. A log fell from the fire with a crackling sound and he woke with a start. "Must have dozed off," he muttered, looking round for Mole.

"Mole," he called. "Mole, old friend, where are you?"

There was no answer. Rat stood up and stretched, and went into the hall where he saw Mole's scarf was missing. Mole had gone out!

Rat carefully locked the door before setting out to look for his friend. Oh, silly Mole. He was sure he had gone to the Wild Wood.

Rat hurried along, trying not to think about the darkness ahead of him, and soon reached the Wild Wood. Bravely, he went on, paying no heed to the sounds of the weasels and stoats, calling loudly and cheerfully, "Mole, are you there? It's me, Rat. Where are you Mole?"

For an hour or more he searched and called, then he heard a faint call. "Oh Rat, is it *really* you?" and he rushed to the beech hollow where Mole was hiding.

"Oh Rat, dear Rat, I am so glad to see you," Mole said. "I've never been so frightened in all my life!"

"It's all right now," said Rat. "But you shouldn't have gone off without me. And you should never have come to the Wild Wood on your own."

"But surely it's not as bad as that," said Mole, who felt braver.

"Oh, for animals like Otter and Badger, it's fine," said Rat, "but not for you."

23

"What about Toad?" asked Mole. "I don't suppose he's scared of the Wild Wood."

"Toad!" Rat laughed. "He wouldn't show his face here for a hundred pounds!"

Rat knew they had to get away from the Wild Wood as quickly as possible. "Come on then, Mole," he said, "we must make tracks for home, it's getting late and we don't want to get lost."

So Rat stepped out of the tree, only to step back again at once.

"What is it?" asked Mole fearfully.

"It's snowing," said Rat. "Snowing hard."

Mole peeked out and saw that the whole wood had changed. Everything that had scared him—trees, logs, branches, holes—had all gone. All were nestling under a thick carpet of sparkling snow, and the flakes that fell silently, filling the air, seemed to tingle on his face.

"Well, come on," said Rat. "The snow's a nuisance, but no sense in hanging about. Best get on."

Rat and Mole set off through the snow-covered wood. Soon Rat had to admit he was lost. "Let's make for this dell down here," he said. "We can have a rest and maybe the snow will stop after awhile."

So, slowly and carefully, their feet making patterns in the snow, Rat and Mole went into the dell. Suddenly, Mole tripped and fell.

"Oh, oh, oh!" he cried. "I've hurt my leg." And he sat in the snow and rubbed his leg with his paws.

"Poor old Mole," said Rat. "Let's have a look. Oh dear, you have got a nasty cut. I'll wrap my hankie round it."

"I must have tripped over a stump," wailed Mole. "Oh, it does hurt."

"Soon be all right," said Rat, tying his hankie firmly round it. "Funny, you might think it had been cut by something sharp," and he looked around. Then he gave a shout. "Oh, come and see what I've found!"

Mole limped towards him and found Rat staring at a door scraper. He must have tripped over it in the dark.

"Mole, don't you see what I see?" asked Rat. "Oh, you are silly sometimes," he said impatiently. "It means there is a *door* very close by!"

Why hadn't he thought of that? Mole hung his head. Rat poked

about with a loose stick he found and scraped away at the snow.
"Look!" he cried, and there in front of him was a door. Not just *any*
door, but a smart door with a bellpull. They had found Badger's
house!

Mole was delighted. "Oh Rat, you are clever," he said, but Rat was too busy ringing the bell to listen to him.

After a long time, they could hear feet plodding along the passage and at last the door opened and Badger stood looking out at them.

"Who is it?" his gruff voice asked. "Who is ringing my bell at this time of night?" He sounded very cross.

"Badger, *dear* Badger, it's me, Rat. Let me in. My friend Mole has cut his leg and we lost our way in the snow."

"Why, Ratty old chap, come in, come in," said Badger in a friendly voice, opening the door wider so that a rush of warm air came to meet them. "Come in Rat and your friend, er Mole, too."

So they followed Badger into his home and down a long, long tunnel. Mole was just the tiniest bit scared of Badger. He seemed so big. He was wearing a long, thick dressing-gown and slippers, and carried a tall candlestick in his paw.

"Come along in," said Badger. "There's a fire to warm you and lots of food. It's no night to be out, but you always did get up to tricks, Ratty."

Soon Rat and Mole had joined Badger in a large kitchen with a

roaring fire in the range. It smelt warm and there were two comfy chairs on either side. "Warm yourselves," said Badger, "while I get you some soup. Nothing like soup to warm you up on a cold night."

He filled a big saucepan and gave it a stir while he took plates from the dresser in the corner.

"Sit yourselves down and tuck in," said Badger, setting steaming plates of hot soup in front of them at the long table in the centre. "Help yourselves to bread and anything else you want."

"Best make it an early night," Badger said presently, "we have all day tomorrow to talk. You can tell me all the news then." He showed Mole and Rat to their rooms, and both of them were so tired they fell asleep at once.

Next morning Mole had a surprise when he went into the kitchen as Badger called him for breakfast. Two hedgehogs were already sitting at the table eating porridge!

"Good morning, Mole," said Badger. "I hope you slept well. Pay no heed to our young friends, they come every day. Sit yourself down and make yourself at home." And he set a large bowl of porridge in front of Mole.

There was no sign of the snow melting, so Rat and Mole stayed with Badger in his warm sett for a few days. One morning Badger asked, "How's Toad these days?" He always liked Toad, even if he was silly.

"You may well ask!" said Rat. "Toad's impossible since he bought that car!"

"Oh, so he's got a car has he?" said Badger. "Didn't know he could drive."

"Oh, he can't drive," said Rat, "but that makes no difference. He drives too fast everywhere, and he's had lots of crashes already. He's been in hospital three times and been fined in court more than once but goes on doing it."

"He sounds a menace," murmured Badger, looking at the flames.

"Yes, he ought to get someone to drive him around, someone who *can* drive, but he won't listen if you tell him. The fines don't worry him either with all his money."

"That's part of the trouble, I should say," said Badger. "Toad's rich and he'll be killed or ruined, one or the other." And he shook his head.

All three animals stared into the fire, each lost in his own thoughts. There was no hope for Toad it seemed, and he was their friend.

One morning Otter came. "I thought I'd find you here," he said, shaking water all over the carpet. "The snow's melting and the riverbank is flooded. We looked for you both as Rat's house is full of water, and then I thought you must be with Badger. No sign of you at Toad Hall."

After Otter had gone, Rat sat and thought about his house. He wanted to get back as soon as possible.

"Come and see the rest of my house before you go," said Badger to Mole. "It is so deep down, it never gets flooded." And he took Mole all over his lovely sett for he was proud of the way the tunnels ran for miles underground.

"Did you dig *all* this?" asked Mole in amazement.

"Oh no, bless you," said Badger laughing, "it's taken years to build. My grandfather started it, and all of us have added rooms over the years."

Rat and Mole said goodbye to Badger and set off through the Wild Wood towards their home on the riverbank. Rat was in a hurry and took long strides so poor Mole had to scamper along to keep up with him. Suddenly, he stopped and gave a yell.

"Rat, wait, just a minute," but Rat didn't hear and ran on. Mole was sure he had found his old home and he just wanted to take a look. "Rat, *please*," he wailed, tears running down his cheeks, and Rat turned in surprise.

"Why, what's the matter?" he asked coming back.

"This is where I used to live," sobbed Mole. "Please let me look at it, just for a minute."

"Of course, why didn't you say so," said Rat helping Mole to brush away some of the snow. At last they found a small front door. Mole jumped up and down in great excitement.

"It's my house," he cried, "come in." He pushed open the door and Rat followed him inside. All was spick and span except for a layer of dust, and as soon as Rat saw how much it meant to his friend, he helped him to light a fire and search in the cupboards for some food.

"We'll stay a few days," he said. "Give my place a chance to dry out."

Mole proudly showed Rat over his little home and Rat said how it was just the right size with the little bunk beds. Mole was just a teeny bit ashamed of his plain white plates, but Rat said nothing. He planned to give him some special Mole plates for his birthday.

The two friends were snug and warm in Mole's house and there was plenty of food, especially Mole's favourite tins of sardines.

One night as they sat by the fire, they heard a faint scuffling of

tiny feet and a subdued mutter of voices.

"What's that?" asked Rat, jumping up.

"Oh, it must be Christmas!" exclaimed Mole, clapping his paws in delight. "Open the door, it's the fieldmice come to sing carols."

And as Rat opened the door he could see eight little fieldmice standing in a circle round the door, scarves round their necks, paws in pockets for warmth and feet shuffling. Two of them held tiny lanterns which gave a faint, flickering light.

"Happy Christmas!" chorused the fieldmice, and without waiting for a reply began to sing carols.

Later, as the singers crowded into Mole's little house and tucked into the coffee and cakes he had offered them, Rat looked at him and said, "This has been a good year." Mole smiled. He thought so too.

The following summer on a morning that was bright and with a hint of the warmth to come, Mole and Rat were up early, busying themselves with the blue and white boat. Rat had decided to re-paint it and they had just finished, and were impatiently waiting for it to dry. Then they could go for a picnic.

Mole was sitting on the riverbank watching as Rat gently touched the sides of his boat with his paw. "Mmmm, almost dry," he said, "best wait another day to be sure."

The two friends went back to Rat's house wondering what they could do with their day. Then there was a knock on the door and Badger was standing on the doorstep as Rat opened it.

"Why, Badger! How nice to see you," he said. "Come in."

But Badger said briskly, "Come along we've work to do!"

Mole and Rat looked puzzled.

"It's Toad," Badger explained. "Otter tells me he has got another, even faster car. Come along, we are off to Toad Hall to put a stop to his foolishness!"

And sure enough outside Toad Hall was the biggest, shiniest car they had ever seen. Toad was walking round admiring it and wearing the strangest clothes!

"Hello Ratty and Mole," he cried, coming to greet them, "and Badger too! This is an honour! Just in time for a spin in my new red car. Lovely isn't it?"

"Very nice," squeaked Mole, and Badger glowered at him.

Badger looked at the great big red car (Toad loved red) and at Toad who was wearing a flat cap, huge goggles, gaiters, an enormous overcoat and great big gloves on his paws.

"Mr Toad has changed his mind. He doesn't want the car after all," Badger said to the man who had brought the car.

And as the driver, muttering to himself, drove the bright red car away down the drive Badger hustled Toad up the steps into his house.

"Now listen Toad," Badger said sternly when they were inside. "This nonsense has got to stop. No more cars from now on." And as Toad crossly took off his cap, goggles, gloves, gaiters and overcoat, Badger told him that he had come to put a stop to all his foolishness. For a long time he lectured Toad who sat crossly muttering "How *dare* he interfere" when he could get a word in. Never had he felt so miserable. He wanted to be out in his new car, not listening to Badger! Toad began to sob and at last Badger stopped nagging and asked Toad if he would promise never to drive again.

"Yes, yes, anything," said Toad, having no intention of giving up driving.

Badger made Toad repeat his promise not to drive again in front of Rat and Mole who had been pretending not to listen, and then he said, "I am glad you have seen sense at last."

That was too much. Toad shouted at him, "I loved it. I shall *never* stop driving no matter what you say! I'll get another car. So there!"

Badger didn't waste time talking. He took Toad upstairs, locking him in his room. "He'll come round soon," he said. "Leave him alone for a while."

Rat and Mole looked at each other. They knew Toad wouldn't agree easily. They would all stay at Toad Hall for a few days. They kept watch on Toad who was very miserable, refusing to talk to any of them. One day Badger had to go home urgently, and Rat was left in charge.

"Oh Rat, I'm so ill," whimpered Toad lying in bed. "Do please be a kind friend and fetch me a doctor at once. Oh, and a lawyer too. I'm very ill," he said feebly.

Rat looked at him. He did look awful. So he ran off to find the doctor and the lawyer. Mole was still asleep, but Rat did not think of that, Toad was ill and needed help.

Chuckling to himself, Toad leapt out of bed and knotted the sheets to make a long rope. He climbed out of the window and was soon away down the drive and out of sight. Badger was *furious* when he returned, and the doctor and the lawyer were not pleased that Rat had brought them to Toad Hall for nothing.

Meanwhile, Toad, never happier, had reached the village. Outside the inn there was the biggest shiniest red car he had ever seen. It was even bigger than the one he had wanted. It was too hard to resist. He walked all round it. It wouldn't hurt just to *look*. There was no one about. It did not take a minute for Toad to open the door and slip inside, still looking of course.

Without thinking, for he was so happy, Toad pressed the starter. "Prrrm," the motor roared into life, and all the old passion seized Toad. He let off the brake and in a second was speeding away down the road. He was king of the open road, no one could stop him. Faster and faster he went, the car seemed to have wings.

Alas! His happiness was short lived for he crashed and Toad found himself in court facing a very angry magistrate.

"You are a very wicked Toad," he said sternly. "You have stolen a car, driven without thought of anyone else and crashed it. You might have killed someone. This is not the first time."

Toad trembled. It had all gone wrong. He had only wanted fun.

"So, the only thing is to send you to prison," said the magistrate, "for twenty years! Perhaps that will teach you a lesson. Take him away!"

And poor Toad, loaded with chains in case he ran away, was dragged shrieking, saying how sorry he was, he'd never do it again, and shut away in the deepest, darkest dungeon of the castle. Toad shivered and whimpered as the guards pushed him through the doorway of the grim old castle, its spiky portcullis clanging shut behind him.

"Please don't shut me in," begged Toad, but the gaoler took no notice and the door of the dungeon was shut, the key turned in the lock.

For a few weeks Toad gave way to his misery. He refused to eat and sat whimpering in his cell. Why hadn't he listened to Badger and the others? They should have stopped him. But it was all his own fault. And he was here for *twenty* years. The tears rolled down his face.

The gaoler had a pretty daughter who helped her father by taking the food to the prisoners. She felt sorry for Toad who had rudely refused all the prison fare. She loved animals and hated to see him so thin and miserable. So she took him some of her own food and coaxed him into eating it. Toad began to talk of Toad Hall and life in the country with his friends, and the girl grew fond of him. She didn't believe all those stories they told about him, and it was a shame for him to be locked away in that awful dungeon. She had an idea.

"I have an aunt who is a washerwoman," she said, and he rudely interrupted with, "Well one can't always help one's relatives."

"Oh, do be quiet and listen, Toad," the girl said. "I want to help you. My aunt, the washerwoman, comes to the prison every Friday. You are very rich and a few pounds would help her. She would lend you her dress and bonnet and you could escape from this castle pretending to be the washerwoman. It's the only way."

At first Toad scoffed at the idea, but then it began to appeal to him. It was all arranged, Toad giving the washerwoman some golden sovereigns he had hidden in his pockets.

Toad looked just like the old washerwoman as he stepped out through the gates of the prison with a cheery wave to the guard. He felt the teeniest bit annoyed that anyone should take *him* for a washerwoman, then he remembered he had escaped!

He hurried to the station and was just going to ask for a ticket when he remembered he had left all his money in his pockets in the dungeon.

"I've left my purse behind," he said to the man in the booking office. "I'm known round here, so let me have a ticket and I'll send the money tomorrow."

"Be off with you," said the man rudely. "No money, no ticket."

Toad walked up and down the platform tears running down his face. The engine driver saw him and felt sorry for him.

"What's the matter, Mother?" he asked kindly. "Lost your ticket?"

"Yes, yes," said Toad in a feeble voice, "and I must get home to my children, all ten of them."

"Well, I'll help you, if you'll help me," said the driver who was a kind man. "This is a dirty job and my wife hates washing, so if you'll wash a few shirts for me, I'll give you a ride."

"Yes, yes, anything," Toad said, eagerly scrambling into the cab beside him. The guard blew his whistle and waved his green flag and soon they were speeding down the track. Toad was happy, for each mile was taking him further and further away from the prison.

"Faster! Faster!" he called to the driver, who looked at him in surprise.

Then he saw there was another train chasing them, with policemen and prison guards, waving and shouting.

Toad decided to be honest. "Oh please help me, dear kind driver," he begged. "I'm not a washerwoman. I am Toad of Toad Hall and I've escaped from prison and they are chasing me!" And his voice rose in a wail as he thought what would happen if they caught him. He'd be in prison for ever!

"Well, why were you put in prison?" asked the driver.

"It was nothing," said Toad. "I only borrowed a car for a little while. And you know how cross some people get."

The driver looked at him and said, "Well, I don't like cars myself, but you seem to be in a fix, so I'll do my best to help you." And he piled on more coal to make the train go faster. On and on they went, as fast as they dared, with the passengers behind screaming in fear and the other train getting nearer and nearer. It was no use. The driver slowed down and told Toad to jump out and wished him luck.

Toad picked up his skirts and jumped, rolling down a bank while the train rattled away into the distance. He looked around and saw he was near a wood, so, as it was dark, huddled down among the leaves in a hollow tree and fell asleep.

Next day Toad woke up early. He hurried along the edge of the wood and soon came to a canal, sleepily moving along. He heard the sound of a horse's hoofs on the towpath. He watched as it came nearer and passed him to be followed by a long, low barge. A woman in a sunbonnet waved to him as she passed, one hand on the tiller to steer the barge.

"Nice day," she called.

"Lovely," called Toad, running along beside her. "I wonder if you can help me? I'm trying to get to my married daughter who lives near a fine house called Toad Hall, and I've lost my money and I've lost my way." And his voice turned into a wail.

"My! You are in a fix," laughed the woman, "but cheer up. If you want Toad Hall, I'm going that way myself. I'll give you a lift."

She steered the barge close to the bank and Toad, thanking her, climbed aboard. Soon he would be home at Toad Hall with all its comfort! He felt so happy he began to boast about his work as a washerwoman.

"I have the finest business in the country," he said. "I do it all myself, the washing, ironing, starching. I do it all."

"You do *all* of it," said the woman, "*yourself*?"

"Oh yes, I love washing," said Toad, carried away.

"That's a bit of luck," said the woman. "I don't mind washing if I've nothing else to do. But it's like this, my husband has gone off to find a rabbit for lunch, and I'm to pick him up at the next lock. So I'm too busy with the barge to do the washing. You can do the washing for me," she said happily. "There's a tub in the back there, with a kettle and a bucket to haul the water up from the canal. Come along."

"Oh, let me steer," said Toad who had never washed anything in his life.

"Let you steer? No, no!" laughed the woman. "Come along."

Soon Toad found himself surrounded by a pile of washing, and a bar of soap. Of course, he made a terrible mess of it, with soapsuds and water everywhere, and no matter how much he slapped and pushed the washing, it still looked dirty.

"Fine washerwoman you are to be sure," the woman said. "I've been watching you for some time. You are a teller of tall tales!"

Toad's anger boiled over. He was wet, cold and fed up. "How dare you," he shouted, "you low, common bargewoman! I am Toad of Toad Hall. Don't you laugh at me!"

The woman came nearer and peered at him. "Yes, you are a toad," she said. "A nasty crawly toad. And on my barge. Be off with you." And she picked Toad up by a leg and threw him on to the bank. He heard her laughing as the barge moved on and ran after her, bent on revenge.

"Put yourself through the mangle, Toad," said the woman. "You're all wet!" and she roared with laughter.

Toad ran past the barge and untied the horse. Jumping on its back he kicked it into a gallop, leaving the bargewoman shouting in fury as he rode away. After a while he stopped to give the horse a rest and found a gypsy camp, the air filled with the lovely smells of cooking. One of the gypsies looked at him. He could see his nose quivering and knew he was hungry.

"Want to sell that horse?" he asked, piling food on to his plate.

"Sell my horse! The very idea," said Toad. "I'm much too fond of him, he's a special horse." Then his nose wrinkled. That food did smell good and he was terribly hungry. "All the same, how much would you give me for him—just suppose I wanted to sell?"

The gypsy looked at the horse. "Shilling a leg," he said, still eating.

"That's not enough," Toad said. "Not nearly enough."

The gypsy stood up. "Tell you what," he said, "I'll give you five shillings, and that's my last offer."

"If you give me six shillings and sixpence *and* some food, you can have the horse," said Toad.

The gypsy grumbled a bit, but he knew it was a bargain so he agreed, and Toad was soon eating a lovely breakfast. Feeling refreshed, he said goodbye to the horse and the gypsy and set off. He was getting near to his home now and he walked faster and faster. He heard a car coming and stepped out to stop it.

"I'll arrive home in style," he said. "That'll show them I'm still Toad of Toad Hall."

As the car drew nearer Toad recognized it. It was the same one he had stolen from the inn. He fell into the road in misery and the car stopped and two men got out. They lifted Toad gently into the car and asked him if he felt better. They drove on for a few miles and Toad began to feel braver. After all, they didn't know him.

"I am sure I'd feel better if I could sit in front by the driver," he said. So they carefully lifted him on to the front seat and sped on.

Toad began to feel confident. He wanted to drive again. He *must* drive again!

"Do you think I could drive this car?" he asked the driver. "I would so love to tell my friends that I have driven a car, just once!"

The driver laughed and one of the men said, "Oh let her have a try, can't do much harm."

So Toad changed places with the driver and without waiting for any instructions, pressed his foot down and the car leapt forward.

"Careful, Washerwoman!" the driver said, trying to get hold of the steering wheel, but Toad paid no heed, shaking him off and going faster and faster.

"I am no washerwoman," he shouted. "I am Toad of Toad Hall, the Toad who always escapes. No prison can hold me."

"Seize him," cried the men, trying to stop Toad, but he drove on

and sent the car crashing through a hedge to stop in the middle of a pond. Toad was flung out, landing in the middle of a meadow. He looked across and saw the car nearly submerged in the pond and the men clambering out into the water. There was no time to dally, so he picked himself up and ran as fast as his legs would allow across the grass. The men were chasing him and gaining on him. On and on he ran until, with a splash, he fell into the water. He had run straight into the river! The current took him downstream and he clutched at the reeds until he came to a hole. A brown face appeared, whiskers twitching. It was Rat!

Rat pulled Toad into his hole where he shook himself, sending sprays of water everywhere. "Oh Rat, dear dear Rat, am I glad to see you," he said. "You'll never believe all my adventures."

"Come along, get out of those wet things, and you can tell me all about it later," said Rat. "You look just like a washerwoman. Goodness knows what you have been doing. Thought you were in prison!"

Toad looked at himself in the mirror. He *did* look like a washerwoman. Soon he had had a bath and put on some of Rat's dry clothes and was sitting down to lunch with Rat. As they ate, Toad told his friend all his adventures and Rat listened without saying a word.

Then he wiped his whiskers and sat back, looking intently at Toad. "I don't want to upset you after all you have been through," he said, "but don't you see, it's all your own fault! None of this would have happened in the first place if you hadn't been so silly! Badger, Mole and I did our best to help you, but you just went off and took that car. Badger was *very* upset, I can tell you. We all wanted to be your friends, but now who wants to know a *criminal*!"

Toad hung his head. Rat was right. When he thought about it, he knew it was his fault. And all he had wanted was to have fun.

"You're right, Rat old friend," he said humbly, "you're so right. And I'm sick of cars now anyway. I've got a much better idea. What do you think of *motor* boats on the river?"

Rat stood up. He had heard enough. "Oh, Toad," he said, "I thought prison might have done you some good. But it's useless, you're just the same. If it's not cars, then it's something else. Motor boats! I wash my hands of you."

"Oh well, never mind," Toad said cheerfully. "I have had enough of adventures anyway. I'll just live quietly at Toad Hall and be a model to all. My friends will be welcome to come to dinner of course, but no more travelling for me, in cars or motor boats."

"But Toad, don't you know the stoats and weasels have taken Toad Hall?" asked Rat.

"Taken Toad Hall?" repeated Toad feebly. He could not believe it. His lovely home taken by those awful stoats and weasels. "When?" he asked.

"Well," said Rat tactfully, "when you went away after all that fuss over a car." He paused, not wanting to hurt Toad, but feeling he should know the truth. "The animals took sides over it and those in the Wild Wood said it served you right. Mole, Badger, and, it goes without saying, myself, and Otter all spoke up for you."

"Too kind," muttered Toad.

"Well, to cut a long story short," said Rat, "one night a band of weasels, armed to the teeth, crept up the path, while some sneaky ferrets crept through the garden. Then everything happened very quickly. Those horrid stoats took over the backyard and kitchens. It was over in a few minutes, and although Mole and Badger were keeping watch on your home for you, they attacked them and drove them out."

Rat looked at Toad and saw a tear trickling down his face. "I'll drive them out," said Toad. "How dare they take my house!" he blustered, then he stopped. There was nothing he could do. He might as well have stayed in prison.

Toad stayed with Rat for a few days, feeling very sorry for himself. He just had to get back to Toad Hall somehow. He crept along the path and found a sentry who sent him scuttling back to Rat.

Mole was glad to see Toad who was soon boasting of his cleverness in escaping from prison, but Rat said nothing. He hoped Toad had learnt his lesson, but to hear him talk—well!

Badger arrived and welcomed Toad but told him it was no use anyone helping him if he didn't turn over a new leaf. He would just be sent back to prison and never get out again. Toad thought and thought and knew Badger was right, he *had* been very silly. "I'm sorry," he said. "I only wanted to have fun."

He looked so miserable they all believed him. Badger was brisk. "Well, listen to my plan," he said. "You all know my house is full of tunnels, well, some of them go right up to Toad Hall. If we use our heads, we can get into the house and surprise the enemy. It's the only way."

"Tell us what to do," said the others, ready to help.

Badger told them his plan. That night it was very dark, so Mole, Rat and Toad went to Badger's house. He led them along the tunnels and then held up a paw. "Shush," he whispered, "we're under Toad Hall now. Be very quiet. No one must hear us."

Trembling with fear and excitement the others followed him, sticks in their paws, and they could hear the weasels, stoats and ferrets were having a party.

Step by step they crept nearer until at last they emerged into the passage leading to the dining room. The noises were louder now, the enemy was close.

"Now!" thundered Badger, bursting open the door, and they rushed in shouting. It did not take long. Badger was right, the weasels, stoats and ferrets who were cowardly animals, were soon overpowered, but many fled, though Rat and Mole captured a few weasels, making them clean up the mess. Badger chased the rest of them away, squealing, falling, and scrambling over each other. The Hall was quiet and Toad was its master once more.

Badger, Rat and Mole left Toad to his triumph and crept quietly back to their own homes. For a few days no one visited Toad, who was just happy to be home. Then Badger decided to test him. He planned to give a banquet to welcome him home and with Rat and Mole's help, made all the arrangements. Then he told Toad, who clapped his paws.

"Oh, lovely, I'll make a speech and sing a song," he began, but Badger shook his head.

"No, Toad," he said solemnly, "not one song or speech. You must turn over a new leaf or everything will be wasted. Don't you see? If not, no party."

Toad sulked for a while, then he agreed.

On the night of the party all the riverbank animals gathered in their best clothes and were welcomed at the door by Badger, with Rat and Mole at his side.

Toad was wondering what to wear. He had so many clothes. At the back of his cupboard, he saw a plain brown suit he had bought years ago when he planned to try his hand at stalking and did not want to be seen. It was just right. He joined the party, taking a seat at the side. At first no one saw him, then, when they did, they all crowded round. Toad brushed them aside saying it was nothing, and the party was all due to Badger and Rat and Mole. There was a lovely feast, all of Toad's favourite dishes, but he smiled and shook his head when the animals clapped and asked him to sing or even make a speech. He just said, "Thank you." Never had there been such a reformed Toad.

Peace was restored to Toad Hall and the riverbank animals settled down. Badger persuaded Toad to send some money to the bargewoman for her horse, and Toad bought a gold chain and locket with pearls which was carefully wrapped and sent to the gaoler's daughter. He did not forget the train driver, who had a reward. In the evenings the friends would gather to talk, as friends do, but Toad never boasted at all. And whenever he heard a car horn he would shake his head.

He was a much nicer Toad. Whenever he took a walk, sometimes with Rat or Badger or Mole, or even on his own, the animals would smile at him as he passed in his dull brown suit, and he smiled back at them.

As for the weasels, stoats and ferrets, whenever they saw Toad they fled in terror.